Farm Day

Written by
Sarah Toast

Cover illustrated by   Interior illustrated by
Eddie Young   Joe Veno

Louis Weber, C.E.O.
Publications International, Ltd.
7373 North Cicero Avenue
Lincolnwood, Illinois 60646

Permission is never granted for commercial purposes.

Manufactured in U.S.A.

8 7 6 5 4 3 2 1

ISBN: 0-7853-1066-5

PUBLICATIONS INTERNATIONAL, LTD.
Little Rainbow is a trademark of Publications International, Ltd.

"Katie! We're so glad to see you," says Aunt Sally. "So many new animals have come to live on the farm that we haven't had time to name them."

"We're counting on you. You always think up the best names," says Uncle Peter.

As soon as Dad unloads her suitcases
from the car and says good-bye, Katie is
ready to get started.

"Let's hurry to the barn and say good
morning to your new cow," says Katie.
"Brownie is a good name for a cow."

In the milking barn, Aunt Sally sits on a low stool and begins to milk the new cow. "Mooo," says the cow.

"Brownie is not a brown cow," says Katie. "I guess that means there won't be any chocolate milk."

"All cows give white milk," says Uncle Peter. "The milk you buy at the store comes from cows just like this one."

Aunt Sally shows Katie how the cow gives milk. "It doesn't hurt her."

"I think Spots would be a good name for this cow," says Katie.

"Mooo," says Spots.

Uncle Peter feeds the chickens the corn
and grains they like to eat.

"Listen to this little chick. He's trying
to crow," says Katie.

"He's a baby rooster. Soon he'll wake us up at sunrise," says Uncle Peter.

"His name is Early Bird," says Katie.

"Peep-a-doodle-peep," says Early Bird.

"Good morning, Pinto Bean," says Katie to the farm horse. He is an old friend. "We are going to give you some fresh hay to eat and clean your stall."

Up in the hayloft, Katie sees a barn cat that she has never seen before. "Barn cats are not just pets. They have important work to do. They keep mice out of the barn," says Aunt Sally.

"I'll name this striped cat Tiger, and the cat who is helping Uncle Peter should be called Lion."

"Meow," says Tiger.

"Meow, meow," says Lion.

"I don't want to go in the muddy pig pen," Katie says and climbs on the fence. "Pigs are great," says Farmer Bob. "They're recyclers. I feed them leftovers, called slop, and they grow big."

"Mud keeps their skin cool. You like swimming pools. Pigs like mud puddles."

"I'll call the little pig I'm scratching Mud Pie," says Katie.

"Oink," says Mud Pie.

For lunch Katie eats a sandwich made with lettuce and tomatoes from the garden. She drinks a glass of milk from Spots the cow.

Just then a big dog runs into the yard
and puts his paws on the picnic table.
"Who is he, Uncle Peter?" asks Katie.
"I don't know," says Uncle Peter.

Uncle Peter needs to mend the fence around the cow pasture. While her uncle pulls the fence wire tight, Katie tries to think of a name for the big dog.

"All the animals on the farm work, but this dog just wants to play," says Katie. "I'll call you Funny Bones."

"Woof, woof!" barks Funny Bones.

In the farm workshop, Uncle Peter works
on his tractor. A farmer knows how to fix
all the machines on the farm.

"Your tractor has a name," says Katie.

"I call it Green Machine because it plows the fields, plants, and harvests."

Chug-a-rumble-rumble goes the Green Machine.

Uncle Peter and Bob put out grass for
Spots and the other cows. Katie helps.
She feeds grass to a young calf.

"I think her name should be Little Spots," says Katie.

"Moooo," says Little Spots.

The farmers are tired after a busy day. But Katie still has work to do.

"This firefly is called Starlight. This one is Star Bright. And this one's name is Good Night," says Katie.